Rastamouse

and the
Crucial Plan

Livicated to our irie children:
Rebecca, Cheyenne-Lima, Isaac & Honey

First published 2003 by Little Roots
This edition published 2012 by Macmillan Children's Books
a division of Macmillan Publishers Limited
20 New Wharf Road, London N1 9RR
Basingstoke and Oxford
Associated companies throughout the world
www.panmacmillan.com

ISBN: 978-1-4472-1695-7

1 3 5 7 9 8 6 4 2

A CIP catalogue record for this book is available from the British Library.

Printed in China

Rastamouse

and the
Crucial Plan

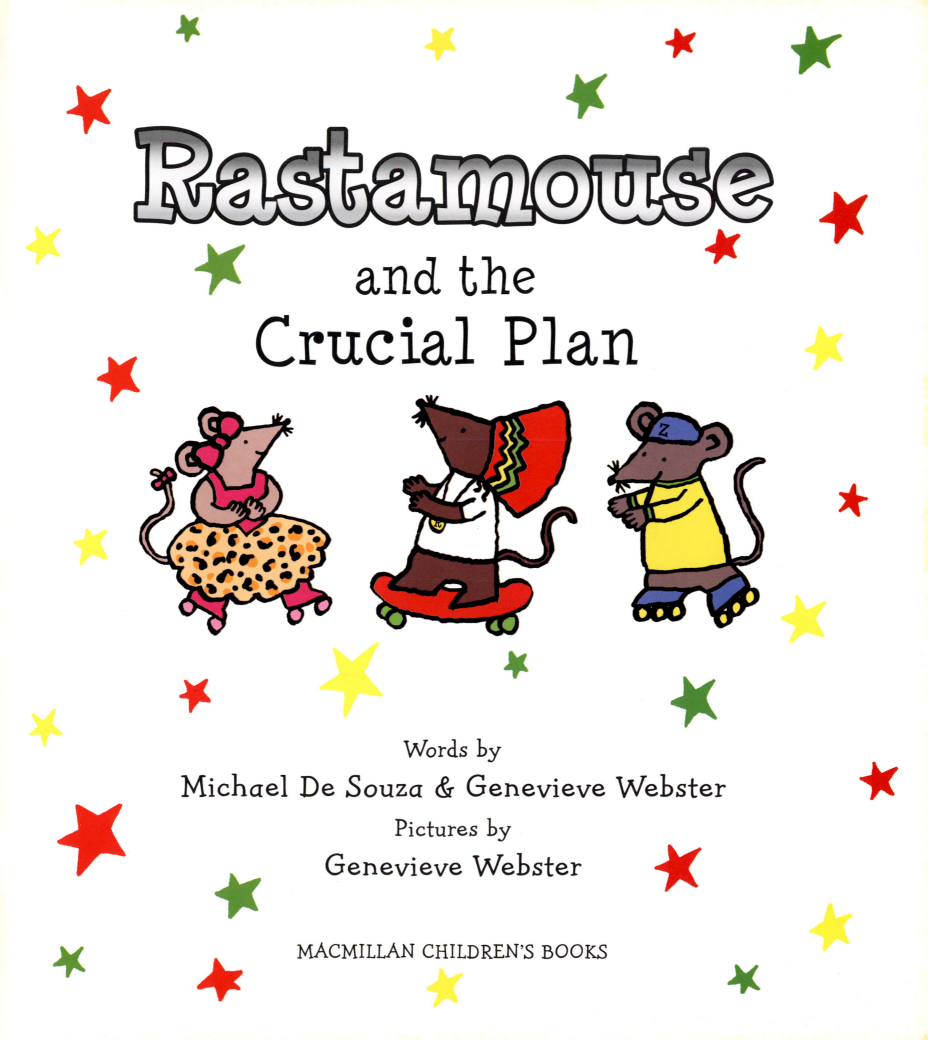

Words by
Michael De Souza & Genevieve Webster
Pictures by
Genevieve Webster

MACMILLAN CHILDREN'S BOOKS

Meet Rastamouse, Scratchy and Zoomer,
Also known as the 'Easy Crew'.
Crime-fighting special agents
With important work to do.

They solve mysteries and have adventures,
They're the best throughout the land.
So cool and brave and funky –
And they play in a reggae band.

They're jammin' in the back yard
When suddenly they hear
An emergency transmission
Through the radio, loud and clear.

"RASTAMOUSE! COME IN! COME IN! ARE YOU READING ME? MESSAGE FROM THE PRESIDENT, COME IMMEDIATELY!"

So off they speed, the Easy Crew,
Straight to the President's house.
No time to jam! No time to waste!
He's a very important mouse.

to the PRESIDENT'S

Wensley Dale, the President,
Begins to show the crew
A video of a cheesy thief,
And asks what he should do.

"He goes by the name of Bandulu,
Has a bite out of his ear.
Wears a red and white bandana
And he's making a career . . .

. . . of stealing from the dairies and shops
ALL the City's cheese
I haven't been able to trap him yet
So Rastamouse, help me, PLEASE."

"Me want to catch dis teefin' mouse,
So give me your advice.
He stole de last cheese dat there was
From poor little orphan mice!"

"Dem little mice woke hungry,
It makes me very sad,"
Cried Wensley Dale, the President
"Dis teef is super bad."

Rastamouse agrees to assist.
"Of course I will, irie man."
So he asks the help of the Easy Crew
To work up a crucial plan.

"Yo, Easy Crew, listen up good,
This is how it rest.
Scratchy ya need a city map,
And Zoomer, ya gymnast vest."

Scratchy flies the President's plane,
While Zoomer hangs by his feet.
They flypost the city with party invites
To ensure one reaches the thief.

Cheese Pie Competition Tonight

To gain entry to this party,
An impossible request:
Because a cheesy dish is what you need
To be welcomed as a guest.

And no-one else has any cheese,
No-one ANYWHERE
Bandulu is the only mouse
Who'll be expected there.

As the thief is in his secret den
Wondering what to bake,
With all the delicious cheese he has
There's plenty of things he could make.

When in flies a piece of paper,
It's the word cheese that catches his eye
So he sets to work immediately
To create a spectacular pie.

Cheese Pie
competition
★ =`PRIZE`=
★ A thousand Pounds ★
of Cheese
DRESS CODE: FORMAL

With a dash of divine inspiration,
He slices and crumbles and grates
A creative concoction of cheeses,
Which he puts in the oven to bake.

Meanwhile back at the President's,
Preparations are nearly complete
For a pretend, prize-giving party
That will lure the rotten cheat.

At seven, Bandulu puts on his tux
And straightens his red bow tie,
Looks in the mirror, smiles at himself,
Then goes off to check on his pie.

The pie is ready and so is he
As the taxi whisks him away.
And when he arrives at the President's door,
He feels it must be his lucky day.

With his heart full of pride for his wonderful dish
He steps across the floor,
Quite unaware that his awesome pie
Will prove he's been breaking the law.

When the spotlight falls on Bandulu, he thinks
He's about to receive the prize
For the best and tastiest cheesy pie,
So imagine the crook's surprise . . .

. . . when he doesn't receive a prize at all,
Or the expected acclaim.
As Rastamouse stares him straight in the eye
And asks him to explain.

"Da cheese is gone from everywhere,
So come on, tell us please,
How you create dis irie dish
Dat's clearly made of cheese?"

"OK, it was me, I teef all de cheese.
I promise me nah do it again."
So Bandulu is handcuffed, taken outside
And frogmarched back to his den.

Inside his den is filled with cheese
Of every different sort.
"Who was going to eat all this cheese,
presuming you didn't get caught?"

"Just me, alone," Bandulu replies,
"Me really love to cook,
But me nah have no friends at all,
That's why me ah get fat – look!"

"You'll have to take it back ya know,
Every single piece,
To dem dairy and dem shop and de orphanage,
Den I'll call de police."

Our hero unlocks Bandulu's cuffs
And tells him what to do
"Give back dem cheese to de baby mice,
No-one must do it but you."

As the mice jump up and play around,
One gives the thief's tail a tug,
Then a teardrop falls from Bandulu's eye,
As they queue up to give him a hug.

On seeing the baddy's remorseful look,
Rastamouse has an idea.
If Bandulu can have a change of heart,
Perhaps he could change his career.

So Rastamouse makes a different call,
Direct to Wensley Dale,
And he consents to the crucial plan,
The plan that cannot fail.

So later that day at the orphanage door,
Bandulu is crowned Head Cook,
On condition he ends his thieving ways
And gives up his life as a crook.

Bandulu teaches the orphans to bake
In a patient, happy way.
The mice teach Bandulu how to love
Through their laughter and their play.

"Easy Crew: come in! Come in!
Are you reading me?
A message from the President:
Listen up, you three.

Rastamouse: come in! Come in!
Me loved ya crucial plan.
Thank you for a job well done
Or as you would say, IRIE MAN!"

IRIE

pronounced: i-ree

definition: anything positive or good